On the Wind

On the Wind

One Woman's Journey Through Life

Gladys Dorris

authorHOUSE®

AuthorHouse™
1663 Liberty Drive
Bloomington, IN 47403
www.authorhouse.com
Phone: 1-800-839-8640

Published by AuthorHouse   09/26/2012

ISBN: 978-1-4772-7345-6 (sc)
ISBN: 978-1-4772-7344-9 (hc)
ISBN: 978-1-4772-7343-2 (e)

Library of Congress Control Number: 2012917775

Contents

On the Wind

by
Gladys Dorris

This book would not have been possible without the support of

- my friend and former school principal-superintendent, Jerry Stinson, who gave me confidence;
- my loving husband, John Dorris, who gave me encouragement and inspiration;
- my friends, Gloria Odom and Mary Martha Arana, for their review and recommendations;
- and my friend, Fraron Holik who pre-read and critiqued.

Also, thanks to everyone who inspired the characters and events in this story.

Chapter One
August 1955

A s eight-year-old Kathleen Schmidt lay on her back watching maple keys spin slowly ground-ward on the early August breeze, warm sunbeams sliced through the leaves of the towering hard maple. Kathy, as she was called by her family and occasional friend, watched raptly as the keys mimicked tiny helicopters on the seeds' germination journey thus ensuring new growth in the spring and survival of frigid Canadian weather common in Kathy's mostly-German-immigrant home town.

"Kathy, kommen liebchen, macht schnell!" her mother called from their front porch two doors down. "It's almost time to go." Kathy jumped dutifully to her feet tossing her long, blonde, incredibly straight hair over her shoulders, dislodging the daddy long leg spider from her hair exiling it to the ground.

Kathleen hated to leave. She loved her childhood home even though childhood was a term she couldn't comprehend. Home was comforting because it was familiar and predictable; it didn't mean safety, security, love, or any other amorphous concept that mysteriously separated her from classmates and, thus, from forming any long-term friendships.

Kathleen's best friendship rating belonged to her "older" sister Sharon whose advanced age, one year older than Kathleen, afforded Sharon the respect of one near-adulthood. Even though she was "almost a grown-up," the two girls shared powerful imaginations. They could play for hours launching leaf-sailboats in the puddles formed by rain droplets that dripped from maple trees into depressions alongside the

Canadian Pacific Railway that cut through their small-town neighborhood. Lack of toys never concerned the girls. They never knew anything different and were adept at creating playthings from a small block of wood, empty soup can, piece of string, or almost anything they could find.

Now they were leaving. "Hurry Kathy," her mother called again. "We have to be gone before your father gets home from work." Kathleen couldn't delay any further. She straightened her hand-me-down shorts and faded pink t-shirt and reluctantly hurried home. Sharon was already there, helping their twelve-year-old brother Larry stuff suitcases into their uncle's car. Kathy saw their platinum-blonde hair popping in and out of the car's open trunk. Departure was essential and now appeared imminent. Father had come home drunk again the night before and, predictably, wasted no time beating Larry, leaving him with the usual black eye and purple-black bruises scattered about on his thin, lanky frame. The girls had avoided Father's punishing blows again by hiding beneath soiled laundry in their bedroom closet.

Neighbors averted their eyes in a "see no evil" pretense as Uncle John backed out of the driveway. What happened in the Schmidt house would forever remain in the Schmidt house; knowledge of their family life apparently amounted to "ferboden" knowledge and nobody wanted to be found in possession of it.

*　　*　　*

Ruby had almost no difficulty finding housing for her young family. Their new home was a two-room, second-floor flat in the old, in-need-of-renovation Windsor Hotel. She was pleased that their room encompassed a corner of the building so they could open windows on both outside walls to let the afternoon breeze help keep them cool. The room had one small rotating fan with one broken blade.

Employment was difficult if not impossible for Ruby to find, but she had to somehow support her family. She had dropped out of public school in grade six after losing most of her eyesight due to cataracts and subsequently being declared legally blind. With no marketable skills and very limited sight, she now squinted to decipher the help-wanted ads in the weekly newspaper published in their "refugee town" some two hours distant. Larry was the new dad-of-the-house and took his responsibilities very seriously. He read the ads to her in the Windsor Gazette from his vantage point above her right shoulder.

"Hey, what about this one, Mom? This one says they need a cook right here in this hotel. Everybody knows you're a great cook, and I can watch the girls while you're at work downstairs," Larry volunteered. "What have you got to lose? Go talk to them right now before someone else gets the job. We don't have much money left, Mom." Larry hoped his voice didn't reveal his anxiety. He didn't wish to upset his mother or add any stress to her troubled life. Larry's role as surrogate "man-of-the-house" fell naturally upon his young shoulders like a butterfly net falls naturally upon a trapped Monarch.

*　　*　　*

Ruby's excitement mounted simultaneously with each hurried step as she bounded back up the solid maple staircase. "I got it! I got the job! Everything is going to be okay. I start tomorrow morning," she announced after catching her breath.

Sharon and Kathy looked up briefly from their cutting-dolls-from-the-Sears-catalog project. "That's nice, Mom," both girls said in unison as though they had been practicing their speech for hours.

Larry's questions flew consecutively from his lips, not waiting for any answers. "Who's your boss? Is he nice? Is there more than one cook? What will you have to do? What time do you start in the morning? What kind of food will you be making? How much will they pay you?"

"Slow down, Larry, all in good time," she said. "I'll explain everything later. I am just so relieved to find a job. Right now, I don't care what I cook or even what they will pay me. I can tell you this much though. My bosses are Mr. and Mrs. Gould, and they seem nice."

Thus began the Schmidt's long journey to find their new normal. Security was beginning to creep into Kathleen's life. Safety, however, remained neither viable nor visible.

* * *

For two months, Larry and Sharon enjoyed a time-out from school. Bookworm Kathleen mourned hers. For her, nothing was more enjoyable than school and learning.

She had begun grade one at age five because Sharon did. They were inseparable, so Kathleen had snuck off to school every day following in her big-sister's footsteps. The first couple of days Father was called to retrieve his youngest daughter but was so verbally abusive to Kathleen and the teacher when he had to leave work that, within a week, Kathleen was allowed to remain in class. The teacher soon realized that Kathleen was able to do grade one work.

Because Kathy was one year younger than all her classmates, her educational journey began a full year earlier than the others, including Sharon. Complicating things even further, the school year ended with Sharon failing to pass into grade two; however, Kathleen not only passed into grade two, but on her teacher's recommendation advanced into grade three thus skipping a full grade. Kathleen began the following year in grade three at only six years old. Kathy found something in her life that she could feel good about, her education, and she loved school. Larry and Sharon did not share her love.

Enrollment in school would reveal their location, so Kathleen was missing her most enjoyable pastime, learning—the first two months of grade five. She wondered what the other kids were learning and whether she would be able to catch up with them.

Time passed slowly in their small hotel room despite the girls' creativity and Larry's patience. Uneventful day followed uneventful day followed uneventful day. The Goulds were beginning to question why the children weren't enrolled in school, and Ruby knew that she would soon have to relocate or risk discovery.

*   *   *

The children were startled when someone knocked on their hotel room door about 4:30 one afternoon. Thinking it was probably the hotel clerk coming to collect rent, Larry opened the door and immediately recoiled, jumping back like he was within striking distance of a venomous rattlesnake. His father's large muscular frame almost filled the doorframe, blocking Larry's view of the outer hallway.

"Hi kids. Where's your mother?" Father asked in his best anger-managed voice.

"At work . . . downstairs," Larry stammered. In a knee-jerk reaction, he added, "She gets off work in about twenty minutes," and immediately wished he hadn't said anything at all. The four fell into awkward silence as they waited together and remained silent for a few moments even after Ruby came in exhausted from work.

"Kids, go outside for a while. Your mother and I need to talk." Somehow, Father had lost his usual intrepid tone and it frightened Larry. He didn't know why.

Within an hour, all their belongings were loaded into the family car and they were heading back to their childhood home. The children didn't speak even to each other all the way back. Questions could wait for Mother alone. Asking Father anything was off limits.

Later that night, after the children were in bed and fast asleep, their father went quietly out to the garage, opened the car trunk, removed the shotgun and box of shells and placed them back into the locked cabinet in the corner.

*　　*　　*

Chapter Two
November 1964

Winter storm winds howled mercilessly outside her hometown hotel window as Kathy, soon-to-be-eighteen, snuggled contently in the arms of her husband on her wedding night. Two hours earlier, in her parents' living room, she had said, "I do," to Ken Gould, the son of Windsor Goulds. Susan had looked beautiful in her soft pink maid-of-honor dress she borrowed from a friend. The bride wore the traditional white, a bridal dress she bought brand-new, the first never-worn-before garment Kathy ever had on her body. Her long blonde curls were slightly hidden by a home-made veil held in place by light pink, artificial flowers. She did not have the traditional bouquet of flowers; Kathy barely had enough money to pay for the dress.

The groom looked very handsome in his black rented suit with a single pink silk rose tucked into the lapel. He was tall, slim, dark-haired, hazel-eyed, and five years older than Kathy.

Kathy's father uncharacteristically offered to pay the preacher, and the groom gladly accepted the offer. Kathy never noticed that the Justice of the Peace officiating hurried through the ceremony, or that her father almost smiled when he was asked to give her away.

(Neither Kathy nor Ken remembered ever having met before their blind date six months earlier. In fact, Kathy did not make the connection to the hotel in Windsor until years after their eventual, eventful divorce.)

This night Kathy's mind was filled with romantic images. At the moment, she felt very adult. "So this is how it feels to be a woman," she thought.

He had made her a woman. Kathy never experienced sex before, although they had come close several times. Somehow, she always had enough control for both of them. Ken knew how to excite her passion, and tonight there would be no further need for control. Her emotions screamed to be released with the same intensity the storm pounded out its anger on their windowpane.

Kathy naively never wondered where Ken acquired his bedroom skills. She loved him blindly, accepted his faults, and overlooked whatever she had to. He was her savior. Ken freed her from childhood and was now tutoring her in womanhood. "Life doesn't get any better than this," she thought.

*   *   *

Ken had been with many women, and the most recent was just the night before his wedding to this inexperienced child he now held. "What was I thinking?" Ken almost said it aloud but stopped himself in time. "Kathy can never know," he thought.

They had met on a blind date, fixed up by a mutual friend, and he had taken Kathy first to a chick-flick Elvis movie, then to his apartment. When he kissed Kathy as they were watching television, she suddenly blurted out, "I love you!" She had never been kissed before by anyone, not even by her mother, and she told herself that she must love him. To her, she was in the middle of a storybook romance.

"Are you sure?" Ken asked. He had never been told that by any of his previous conquests, at least not this early in the relationship. "What's going on with this chick? This little girl is going to be easy," he thought and started putting his best moves on her. Then something happened that Ken had never experienced before. Rejection! His advances were stymied, and he found the challenge strangely exciting.

Ken didn't particularly like Kathy's blonde hair or blue eyes; his preference had always been dark hair and brown eyes. He was not attracted to her pubescent body either. Ken loved large breasts and was not bashful about it. Now here he was, married to this child-bride and basking in his private, dubious victory. He had won; he had gotten her into bed.

"Now what?" he thought. "How do I get rid of her?" Ken's sense of conquest, the total obsession that he must bed every female to whom he offered himself, had led him inevitably to this night.

Of course, he blamed Kathy's father for getting him into this conundrum. Her father had witnessed one of their "almost sex" encounters as they huddled in the darkness of the enclosed back porch. His advances had been repelled again, but her father didn't stick around long enough to see it happen. Instead, her dad quietly retreated into the house and said nothing to Kathy about the incident. Ken, however, had not escaped her dad's vehement reaction. Her father did not care about protecting Kathy's virtue; he just wanted Kathy out of his house so she could no longer cost him any money.

Ken resented her father's ultimatum. Ken was simply to either marry Kathy right away in a true "shotgun wedding" or go to jail for statutory rape as Kathy had not yet turned eighteen years old. Therefore, a hasty wedding took place and Kathy was swept romantically off her feet and into Ken's bed. Ken snickered to himself with the thought, "Every cloud has a silver lining."

*　　*　　*

It wasn't long before Kathy's pubescent body blossomed into a rotund baby bump upon which her growing breasts drooped. Unfortunately for Kathy, she was still blonde, still had blue eyes and her roundness was especially unattractive to Ken. The only thing attractive about his bride was her incredibly convenient naivety. Ken found another silver lining by seeking comfort in the arms of other women, many other women, all brown-eyed brunettes with large nondrooping breasts.

*   *   *

When labor pains began, Ken was not at home. When Kathy's water broke, Ken interrupted his "date" long enough to drive Kathy to the hospital. He didn't stay to witness the miracle of his son's arrival, but instead returned to his waiting "flavor-of-the-month" date.

Kathy experienced love, true love, for the first time in her life when she looked into the sleeping, peaceful face of her son. Cathartic, healing love welled up deep within her, a love so profound it hurt, and she cried uncontrollably.

"I promise you, son, to love you always, and you will know what love is." Kathy did not promise to give him safety or security because she still did not recognize the need of these.

"I will name you Mark because your arrival marks the first right change in my life," and she held him close listening to his soft baby breaths. Kathy knew that her husband wasn't pleased with her as a wife, and she wondered why. Maybe her baby, his son Mark, would somehow strengthen their marital bond.

Ken wasn't interested in the child and even convinced himself that he was not Mark's father; he did, however, enjoy the extra attention other women paid him because of the child. Somehow, Ken had grown sexier in their eyes.

* * *

Kathy lived for her son and became essentially a single parent/caregiver. Ken was either working at the local mattress factory or using mattresses in others' apartments. Kathy realized that her marriage was dead and, after four years of trying to make it work, filed for divorce. She could no longer overlook his behavior. Mark needed a stable home and she vowed to give it to him. She never regretted the marriage because Ken had given her the love of her life, her little man Mark. Other than the baby, it was as if their marriage never happened; mentally she "kicked Ken to the curb" and closed the book on that chapter of her life.

Kathy now faced a new challenge, financial security for herself and her family. Although jobs were not plentiful, she had no trouble finding employment. Kathy became the head secretary at a hardware store where she worked five days a week, and she also waited tables at an upper-end steakhouse on the weekends. Kathy earned enough to cover her bills and provide for Mark.

Ken stepped out of their lives; he refused to pay child support and never asked for visitation. Kathy reasoned that one cannot miss what one never had, so Mark would never miss his father. Mark enjoyed playing with the other children at his babysitter's house.

Kathleen's life had not gotten any easier although it had seen many changes. Her no longer pubescent body blossomed into a very shapely, athletic woman's body. As a single woman, she soon realized that heads turned when she entered a room. She enjoyed the attention of other men but had no interest in meeting them. "All men are bastards!" she said to herself and resolved to never look back.

Chapter Three

August 1974

The brisk west wind brought a cooling spray off the Pacific Ocean, causing Kathy's hair to cling to the back of her neck like wet spaghetti. In the near distance, she could hear waves smashing violently into the rocky coastline near Crescent City, California. It was nearly 2:00 in the morning, and she felt refreshed after several hours of driving south from Vancouver, British Columbia.

She shone a flashlight under the open hood as she leaned against the fender and looked adoringly at her new husband, the man inspecting the overheated engine. Nine-year-old Mark slept peacefully curled up on the backseat of their beat-up station wagon. All their remaining worldly possessions were either stuffed into the car's limited space or tied securely to the car's roof. The rest of their possessions, mostly her possessions, were now owned by a Vancouver pawn shop owner. Doug had explained that they needed to travel light, and she accepted his direction. Besides, the money would come in handy for food and gasoline until Doug could find a job.

After five years of struggling to eke out a living on minimum wages, Kathy had abandoned her previous resolve and convinced herself that she was once again in love. She met Doug on a blind date fixed up by Sandra, another waitress at her last place of employment in Kitchener, Ontario. Doug was a 29-year-old auto mechanic, three years older than Kathy, and he swept her off her feet—flowers delivered to the restaurant, inexpensive jewelry, burgers at restaurants where she didn't work, and a Batmobile Tonka toy for Mark. He was, in Kathy's estimation, a sexy, athletically-built hunk.

When he offered to share his life with her, she jumped at the chance.

What he didn't share with her was his prison record. Doug had recently been released from the Kingston Penitentiary where he served his full sentence of seven years for grand theft larceny. While incarcerated, he perfected his con-artist technique under the tutelage of Big Ed, his cellmate.

"It just needs to cool down a bit and we can be on our way again. Sorry, I can't afford a room for us. I know you must be tired," he said and gently ran his hands through her spaghetti-hair.

On our way again. The words echoed in her brain. She had heard them so many times lately. During the six months since she said, "I do," she had been on her way six times—from Kitchener to Aurora—to Kingston—to a small town in northern Ontario—to Hedley, British Columbia—to Vancouver, and now on their way to San Diego, California. He had promised to show her places she had never seen, and apparently was making good on his promise. True to his word, they were once again on their way three hours later.

San Diego was not the land-of-opportunity they expected. Also unexpected were the bed bugs and roaches.

Complicating matters, Doug soon learned that all mechanics in California belonged to a labor union, and ex-convicts were not accepted as members in this union. Money quickly dwindled, and once again they were on their way, this time to Texas, this time in desperation.

As the car's radiator repeatedly threatened to overheat, tensions grew between them. "Could life get any worse than this?" Kathy wondered. She didn't have long to wonder.

*　　*　　*

As the sun rose on their road-weary windshield, Kathy spotted what looked to her to be an oasis, Balmorhea, home of the world's largest natural swimming pool. "Thank you God," she prayed silently. She successfully hid her faith from agnostic Doug and didn't want to give him any more reasons to yell at her. "Please let us find a job and a place to stay so we don't have to be on our way again."

Stopping for a burger at the local café, Doug questioned the local patrons. Kathy was not surprised that the service station needed a mechanic or that the service station owner had a small rent house behind the café. "Thank you God,"

Kathy whispered again. Security seemed restored, and for the first two weeks, life was good.

*   *   *

Security is ephemeral, and Doug took it with him when he left Kathy, sneaking out in the middle of the night. Mark woke her in the morning. "Where's Doug?" he asked. "The car is gone. Did he go to work today? I thought today was his day off."

They were abandoned, deserted ironically "in a desert," Kathy thought. She steeled herself against her situation. "What now, God? What do I do now?" she prayed. "I have to protect son," she thought.

She assessed her situation and remembered that she had five dollars tucked in the back of her wallet for laundry. She quickly found it. "Okay," she thought. "I have enough for two burgers and the rent is due. I have no phone and no car. Whatever I do, it must be done right here in Balmorhea."

The café, grateful for the extra help, gave her a job and a line of credit for meals until her first paycheck. Her landlord agreed to wait for the rent too. Once again, Kathy found herself thanking God. Kathy took the overnight shift and, since her rent house was within a stone's throw of the café, Kathy didn't need a babysitter.

In reality, the café was a Mom and Pop operation, a little more than a burger/coffee shop with a four-seat bar and three square tables covered in red and white oil cloth that seemed to suffer from long-term abuse. The entire place could accommodate only sixteen locals or road-worn travelers at one time.

Kathy fell into a day-to-day pattern of work—home—sleep, work—home—sleep, work—home—sleep. Her life became a repetitious pattern of customers—coffee black, iced tea, Dr. Pepper—she knew what they wanted even before they took a booth. One coffee-white cowboy caught her attention, partly because he always tipped two dollars for his one dollar cup of coffee, partly because he came in every night around 11:00 and stayed until 12:00 or later. Mr. Coffee-White was tall, dark and handsome in Kathy's eyes. He always wore Wranglers, cowboy boots and hat. Sometimes he still had on his spurs. Several times she caught him watching her as she carried plates of food to the tables or offered coffee refills from the glass carafe. He reminded

Kathy of a cowboy she saw pictured on the cover of *Western Horseman*. The man made her feel a little uneasy, but most of the time she was too tired to think about him or even to pay much attention.

Coffee wasn't the only thing he liked white. Joe was fascinated by Kathy's blonde, almost white hair. Two months and roughly five dozen cups of coffee-white later, he finally got up the courage to ask her out. He promised to take Kathy and Mark to Fort Stockton, and she jumped at the opportunity to get out of town for a few hours.

* * *

"Not no, but hell no!" Kathy almost yelled at coffee-white Joe the first time he asked her to marry him. "I will not marry you! I will not marry ever again," she explained. "I've been there twice. It isn't fun!" She repeated her answer almost verbatim each of the ensuing five times he asked her. Number seven brought a different response.

She knew she felt something for the cowboy but didn't recognize the feeling. "Look, I'll agree to marry you under one condition," she told him.

"What is it?" Joe couldn't believe Kathy was finally considering accepting his proposal.

Realistic, life-hardened, no longer romantic, Kathy chose her words carefully, soberly, as if she was negotiating a hostage release. "I have been married twice before, so I must be doing something wrong. I don't know what it is," she paused briefly, thoughtfully. "If our marriage doesn't work because of me, I will leave with what I brought into the marriage, my son and my clothes. If it doesn't work because of you, I will take you to the cleaners," she explained. Joe readily agreed. "He must really care about me," she thought. Kathy accepted his proposal.

Mark accepted Joe's proposal too. He wasn't sure if he wanted a father or what a father was, but thought it might lead to toys.

* * *

Kathy nervously went with Joe to meet his parents. "They can't possibly approve of me," she thought. "He's their only child, and I'm sure they have a fixed idea of what their daughter-in-law should be like. I am a twice-divorced, uneducated foreigner with a ten-year-old child!" She was on the verge of tears when Joe opened the door. Kathy fought to control her fight-or-flight instinct.

Joe's mother, Joan, met them at the door, and Kathy's nervousness immediately faded. She greeted Kathy warmly, threw her arms around her and welcomed her to their home. Kathy loved Joan's snow-white hair which was professionally-curled and hairspray-lacquered. "That hair will never be messed up by Texas winds," she thought.

Joan was a retired primary school teacher and related to the world as though everyone was in her third grade classroom. She had the confident air of someone who is always right, and Kathy immediately liked her. If Joan was thinking anything negative, she never let it show. Kathy felt accepted for the first time in her life.

Joe's father, Ken, entered the room from an outside back door. He wiped motor oil from his hands with one of Joan's discarded cup towels, and stuck one out to shake Kathy's hand. He too greeted her warmly, but with a little skepticism. Kathy thought, "He doesn't like me."

Joe was resolute in dealing with his parents and the wedding plans began. Joe and Kathy would be married in two weeks in the living room of his parents' house by the family's minister.

*   *   *

"In a few minutes, your mama is going to marry our son, and we will be your grandparents," Joe's mother explained to ten-year-old Mark in Joe's childhood bedroom. "We're going to love you, and you will have a good life. Joe wants to get you a horse and we are looking for a saddle. We are so happy to have you in our lives."

In what he hoped was his best big-boy voice, Mark responded, "Humph, Joe ain't gettin' no bad deal neither!"

"What?" Mark's straightforward self-confident tone startled her.

"My mom's an experienced wife!" Mark obviously was very proud of his mother.

*   *   *

At the same moment, in her new mother-in-law's bedroom, Kathy did something she had not done before either of her previous marriages. Wearing her blue, cowboy-style dress she had made herself on a portable sewing machine she borrowed from Joan, Kathy knelt beside the twin bed. "Please God, be a guest at my wedding. I am going to need all the help I can get."

* * *

Chapter Four

November 1980

*J K*athy finally had it all—love, security, and safety in Joe's arms, the life she had always dreamed of having. Her new home, a virtual mansion to her, was in reality a small frame cabin nestled at the base of a mountain roughly twenty miles south of Balmorhea. The mesas, hills "without tops," surrounding her home fascinated Kathy. In her imagination, God had sheared off the hilltops and carried them away. "He must have dropped a few tops," she reasoned to explain the out-of-place smaller mesas. Kathy spent her days contentedly cooking, cleaning, gardening, sewing, canning preserves and helping Joe with the ranch chores. She loved her new hobby, oil-painting landscapes, and worked at it every chance she got. Kathy discovered that she had an innate artistic talent.

Joe spent his days feeding, horseback riding, roping, branding cattle and thanking God for bringing Kathy into his life. He loved watching her blonde hair blow in the indomitable Texas winds; Joe was fascinated that her hair became even blonder under the intense summer sun. For Joe, his long romance-drought was over.

Mark stayed busy with his schooling even though he did not inherit his mother's love of learning. Kathy could see her brother Larry's idiosyncrasies in Mark. Each morning Kathy drove Mark two miles to the highway where he caught the school bus. Mark was usually back home by 5:00 in the evening, so he could help his new stepfather with evening chores. At first, Mark took to being a cowboy like a sow takes to a saddle, but eventually he loved his new life on the ranch. Slowly Mark morphed into a Texan.

Joe adopted Mark about the same time that Kathy and Mark became naturalized American citizens, and she never looked back. After the ceremony, Kathy told the presiding judge that she may not be a native Texan, but she got here as quickly as she could. Her only regret was never going to college, but eventually, even that dream became possible.

*   *   *

"Mom, Dad, I want to go to Sul Ross State University in the fall," Mark announced during breakfast. He was about to graduate high school but didn't have any definite plans for his future. "I want to go, but I'm not ready to move out just yet. I am thinking about commuting, if that's okay with y'all."

Joe and Kathy both agreed, but later, after Kathy had time to think about it, she told Joe, "If that pickup goes to college, I want to go too. What do you think, Joe?" Before long, Kathy and Mark were registering for classes; Kathy, now in her mid-thirties, began college with her eighteen-year-old son.

"Please don't tell anyone you're my mother," Mark begged, mortified that others would think he was a sissy for going to school with his mother. Kathy understood and agreed.

*   *   *

"The sky sure looks strange this morning," Mark told his mother one morning as they headed south to school. "I have never seen the sky look so green before."

Kathy remembered Joe cautioning her about West Texas weather. He had explained about tornadoes, how quickly they can form and what to do in an emergency. She had never seen a tornado, but was confident that she would recognize one just as certainly as she had recognized the first Mojave rattlesnake she ever encountered. Joe had rescued her and killed the snake, but he was at home, not with her now.

Within minutes the sky became a black, rolling monster roaring overhead. As quickly as she could pull over, Kathy and Mark sought safety in a culvert below the highway. Instinctively, they lay face down in the gravel and tall weeds, protecting their heads with their hands, just as a locomotive thundered over them. Large hailstones pummeled the surrounding mesquite and cedar bushes and their 1974 Ford pickup. As the funnel tore the world apart above her head, Kathy heard what sounded like several Coke cans crunching and a windshield shattering as her pickup, sucked up by the funnel, was discarded in the ditch near them like a Styrofoam cup tossed by a motorist.

As if in shock, neither spoke for a few minutes. They lay still quietly praying until the tornado's caboose was a safe distance away. "Are you alright, Mark?" Kathy was relieved to hear his voice.

"Yeah, I'm okay Mom. How 'bout you?"

*   *   *

Joe arrived even before the emergency vehicles. He had seen the approaching funnel cloud, called the sheriff and rushed to protect his family. He found them looking very forlorn but unscathed except for a few minor cuts and scrapes. "Thank God you are okay," he said as he hugged them both.

"Sorry 'bout the pickup," Kathy sobbed. "Will insurance cover it?" She feared they might have to postpone college until they could recover financially.

"Yeah, we're okay. I'm just so glad you're okay, honey." That was all he ever said about the hardship of losing his favorite, uninsured, only-two-payments-left pickup.

*   *   *

School resumed like the tornado never happened.

Mark avoided taking the same classes as his mother as much as possible, but eventually the dreaded schedule conflict arose. Mark hated having to take some classes with his mother. Like proximity mattered, his mom always chose a desk close to the front as though she could absorb learning faster. In contrast, Mark cowered in the back and pretended he didn't know that returning, nontraditional, "nerdy" woman at the front of the class even though the family resemblance was obvious to everyone in the room except him. Mark had his mother's cobalt-blue eyes, blonde hair, crooked smile, slender hips and easy gait.

He puzzled over his mother's apparent popularity among his-age-group classmates. Mark had no idea the younger students were taking advantage of his mother's well-honed note-taking skills. She provided them with copies of her notes and even spell-checked and grammar-checked their assigned papers.

Day-after-day, his classmates crowded around her in the cafeteria between classes, inadvertently keeping Mark at bay in self-imposed exile for several weeks. Usually at a table in the corner, Mark ate his lunch alone while he surreptitiously, jealously watched his mother. He couldn't risk revealing the truth; his mother not only attended college with him but she was obviously more popular with what-should-have-been-his friends! "What's the deal?" he asked himself.

One day, when he couldn't stand it anymore, Mark nervously sauntered over and joined his mother's entourage. "That went very well," he told himself. "What was I so worried about?" Mark fell naturally into the conversation with everybody like he had been there all along.

Mark never knew that his classmates were taking bets on how long it would take him to come out of his self-adjudicated "don't know my mother" jail.

*   *   *

Chapter Five

August 1987

"I love sitting out here with you in the evenings," Kathy said resting her head on Joe's shoulder. They gently rocked in their weather-beaten, wooden swing-bench on the front porch of their Pecos County ranch house. They had moved here after the death of Joe's aunt and uncle so Joe could tend to his uncle's Ace Reid cattle. Joe jokingly called the cows Ace Reid cattle because they resembled Reid's half-starved, bony cartoon depictions.

Kathy loved Joe's quirky sense of humor. She also loved the way he filled out his Wranglers. To her, his western "get-up" of boots, spurs, chaps and cowboy hat were equivalent to a movie star in a tuxedo. She thought he must be the sexiest man in all of Texas.

The normally turbulent Texas winds had subsided with the setting of the sun, and the breeze now gently blew her long tresses across Joe's cheek. He loved her hair as much as he loved her, and he unconsciously ran his fingers through it. "I love sitting out here with you too," he said. "Hope your new job doesn't keep us from spending time out here together."

"Oh! Joe," I am so excited about my job," she almost jumped to her feet. "I can hardly wait!" She had taken an English teaching position at Fort Stockton High School and the students would be in class in only seven days. "Can you believe it? I've always loved school but never dreamed that I would become a teacher." To Kathy, teachers were virtual fountains of knowledge, almost holy beings worthy of reverence. "Oh, Joe, I am so happy." She envisioned that she had now become a member of this holy-teacher society, accepted into an exclusive club, an inner-circle of educators.

Joe hoped she wouldn't be too disappointed. His mother and aunt were both retired teachers, and Joe knew how exhausting the challenges of teaching could be. He also knew that teachers could be mercenary, that self-preservation had been an inherent, unwritten rule of survival in the classroom.

He secretly worried about Kathy's language barrier; he knew that even though Kathy spoke English all of her life, she sometimes failed to grasp the nuances of Tex-Mex English. Joe remembered one bitter cold winter day shortly after they married that his mother asked Kathy for a toboggan and the ensuing confusion. From the best that he could surmise, the conversation had gone something like this—

*   *   *

"Kathy, do you know where Joe keeps his toboggan? It's really cold out there."

"Toboggan?" Kathy asked and quickly looked out the kitchen window. "Is it that cold out there? Do you think it's going to snow?" Kathy's excitement grew when her mother-in-law assured her that it definitely could snow. Since Kathy had always loved riding her toboggan down the snow-covered hills in Canada, she was thrilled to think that life in Texas was not going to be so strange after all. She envisioned Joe, Mark and herself having hours of fun on those strange-looking hills around her house.

"But it'll have to snow a lot so we don't high-center on those rocky hills," she beamed. "Does it snow that much in Texas?"

"What? What? What are you talking about? I need Joe's toboggan!" Her normally non-existent anger startled Kathy. "Where does he keep it?" Joan's ears were stinging from the bitter cold wind, and her patience with this foreigner was wearing thin.

"I didn't know Joe had a toboggan, but I imagine he'd keep it in the shed, wouldn't he?"

Like a seething volcano, Joan seemed to erupt. "I need a toboggan! A toboggan! A toboggan!" she repeated it louder each time as if somehow Kathy would understand her better at higher decibels. Adding to Kathy's confusion, her mother-in-law began wildly gesticulating with her arms, repeatedly raising and lowering them above her head with her fists clenched and jerking them angrily back down close to her head with each pronouncement of the word toboggan.

*   *   *

Joe had never seen his mother so upset. He smiled to himself as he recalled seeing her almost in tears, stomping out the kitchen door without the requested toboggan and leaving his new bride totally perplexed. Later, Kathy explained to Joe that what his mother asked for was known as a toque to her.

*   *   *

Choosing what to wear the first day of school took several hours for Kathy. She wanted to look perfect—not too old or too young, not too fancy or too plain, not too bright, or too dull. Joan helped her choose the turquoise shirt-dress with a cloth-covered belt. She also loaned her a diamond drop necklace and stud earrings. Kathy wore her hair tied back with a matching turquoise ribbon. Her shoes had to be freshly polished, so Joe did that for her. Because he didn't want his own trepidation to scare Kathy, he never shared his fears with her.

Joe was right to be concerned about Kathy's lack of Texas language skills. Within the first week of her teaching career, she had another open-mouth-insert-foot moment, this time in the classroom. Kathy came home in tears, totally embarrassed.

"Joe," she said, "you will never believe what happened today. I made a mistake grading a paper. I was writing in pencil but couldn't find a pencil with a rubber on it, so I asked the class if any of them had a rubber."

"What?" Joe asked. He couldn't suppress a smile. "What happened then?"

"They all just sat there, looking at me with deer-caught-in-the-headlight eyes." She continued, "So I asked them again."

"What happened then," Joe by this time was grinning broadly.

"A boy at the back of the room said that he had one, so I asked him to give it to me. I told him that I needed it."

"Um, what did he do then?"

"He asked me if I was sure about that and what was I going to do with it. I told him that I would give it right back to him after I used it. He said that if I used it, I could keep it. He didn't want it back."

Joe could not suppress his laughter. "Then what happened?"

"Well, he stood up and walked really slow to my desk. He had a strange look on his face, and all the other kids started laughing. I thought they were making fun of me, Joe," she continued. "But Joe, you know what? He reached for his wallet! I thought that was a strange place to keep a rubber. Then it dawned on me! Joe, that boy was about to give me a condom. I remembered that some people in Canada call them rubbers too, so I stopped him before he opened his wallet and told him that I thought we had a failure to communicate."

"Honey," Joe tried to stop laughing. "What you needed was an eraser."

* * *

Word of Kathy's faux pas soon circulated among the other teachers, and the mercenaries circled their wagons even before Kathy could learn all of their names. The verdict was in. Kathy was just too different. Before the figurative ink was dry on Kathy's application, her coveted membership in the Holy Teacher Society was denied. She would not be included in any lunch get-togethers and the teachers' lounge would become a virtual vipers' pit for her. Each day, conversation stopped when she entered and resumed when she left.

Chapter Six
April 1995

One summer while Kathy was out of school, she thoroughly impressed Ken with her ability to handle a hammer when she enthusiastically helped her father-in-law build a deck onto their ranch house. "She's going to be okay," Ken thought to himself. "I think Kathy's a pretty good hand," he later told Joe. "She did everything I asked her to do, and she's no stranger to hard work." Joe recognized that this was high praise coming from his Depression-era father. He remembered his father's skepticism when he had first taken Kathy home to meet them.

Kathy was unaware that she had stolen her father-in-law's heart. She only knew that she liked him. Unlike her own father, she could talk to Ken, and he talked to her. Kathy respected him immensely. He brought Joe into this world, and Kathy couldn't imagine life without Joe. Besides, he was such a super grandfather to Mark.

One afternoon, when they took a break from working on the deck, Kathy remembered that she had to take a pickup payment to the bank, and Ken offered to drive her into town. Kathy preferred to have someone else do the driving even though she was a good driver herself. When they pulled into the bank's parking lot, she was surprised when Ken said, "I'm goin' in there with you."

Kathy silently handed the payment to a surly-looking, moustache-wielding, unfriendly teller. After the teller took her check and stamped the payment book, he shoved it quickly back at her without even a smile.

"Are they always like that to you?" Ken asked as they left the bank.

"Like what?" Kathy didn't understand.

"They never spoke to you!" Ken was clearly suppressing his anger.

"I guess they are always like that. I don't remember them ever talking to me," Kathy said softly and wondered why that would upset him. Ken was quiet all the way back to the ranch and didn't get out of the pickup when he dropped her off at the house. He said that he had something he had to do at home, but he would be back in about an hour.

True to his word, Ken was back in an hour and asked Kathy to go back into town with him. He needed her help with something. Kathy wondered what was up when she found herself back at the bank. She had assumed Ken needed some more lumber or nails and expected the destination to be the lumberyard. "Where's the manager?" Ken asked. "I want to talk to him!" his voice was firm and a little louder than necessary.

The manager stood as Ken and Kathy entered his office, and he stuck his hand out jerkily like a robot to shake Ken's hand. Ken ignored the hand. "This is my daughter-in-law,

Kathy, and your people are very rude to her." His voice surprised the manager, and before the man could respond, Ken asked, "How much do my son and Kathy owe on their pickup? I intend to pay it off right now, and we'll not be doing business with your institution ever again." Kathy was speechless, silently observing the conversation as though she was a part of the office wallpaper.

The man quickly began to click-click-click-click on his computer keyboard. He was obviously confused and couldn't remember ever seeing either of them before today. "Who is this girl?" he wondered, but soon found her name in the computer client list. "It looks like they have a balance of $12,476 on their pickup."

"I didn't ask you that," Ken said. "I want to know the pay out right now, today. What does it take to get you out of their lives?"

The man's face flushed as he looked again quickly at the computer screen. "The pay out today is $10,540."

Ken immediately wrote the check, tore it deliberately from his check book, and pushed it toward the manager the same way that the teller had returned Kathy's payment book to her. "I expect you'll mail the title to them as soon as possible.

Goodbye," he began saying as he stood up and finished as they reached the front door. That afternoon, Kathy knew for sure that she belonged; she was a part of their family and could not be any happier.

* * *

The first indication that Ken was sinking into the oblivion of Alzheimer's began just three years later. Kathy and Joe cooked the Thanksgiving turkey and took it to Joan and Ken's house where several friends also came and brought desserts. Like the yummy Thanksgiving smells, laughter and conversation seemed to fill the house, that is, except for Ken who shunned his son most of the day. Whenever Joe tried to talk with Ken, he looked away and refused to speak. Puzzled, Joe waited until the friends left before he asked, "Daddy, you've been mean to me all day. Have I made you mad? What's the matter?"

"I am so mad at you, son, I can't stand it!"

"Why, what have I done?"

Ken's voice cracked with emotion. "You have that nice, young, skinny wife at home, and you brought that fat, old girlfriend over here," he said as he pointed toward Kathy seated in the next room. Ken remembered Kathy as a slim, young woman, not as the slightly overweight "schoolmarm" model she now was.

As the disease progressed, he sank deeper into himself and had to be placed in a nursing home. One day after school, as Kathy was feeding him his supper, he announced, "I guess your mother-in-law doesn't even own a broom."

"Whatever do you mean, Ken? Joan keeps the house very clean. She's an awesome housekeeper."

"I never did get to have a ride on it!" he announced. Then, as if that was all there was to say, he grew silent and said nothing more that day, or ever. He passed away peacefully in his sleep that night. Planning the funeral of your spouse of more than half a century was too much for Joan to bear. Her heart gave out and she joined him in death the next evening, alone in her big four-bedroom house. She had refused Kathy's offer to stay with her that night.

*　　*　　*

During the graveside service, Joe held Kathy's hand as they sat stoically together in front of twin steel-gray caskets and forced back their tears. As though heaven wept the tears they would not allow themselves to cry, heavy rains fell on the canopy and their many friends who refused to leave the graveyard before Joan and Ken were laid to rest.

Later, after the rain had stopped, the caskets were lowered into Mother Earth, and all their friends were gone from the graveyard, Kathy whispered in Joe's ear, "You know, they were my parents too. Thank you for sharing them with me."

*   *   *

Without Ken and Joan, Kathy felt a void in her life and decided to return to college during the summers. She enrolled in Sul Ross again, this time to work on her Master's degree. She reasoned that she spent nine months of the year behind the teacher's desk, and now it was time to spend a couple months in front of it, in a student's desk. She had transitioned into a life-long learner.

Chapter Seven
June 2011

Kathy retired from teaching, or as she referred to it, "gave it back to them." At age 64, she just had "enjoyed about all she could stand" and looked forward to staying at home and helping Joe on the ranch. She retired in the midst of the worst drought locals had ever seen even though Pecos County is on the northern edge of the Chihuahua Desert and Texans are no strangers to dry spells.

The drought-starved tobosa, grama and threeawn grasses remaining in the pastures were in actuality dry straw, rich fodder for wildfires. All that kept the fires at bay was a catalyst—a lit cigarette tossed carelessly by a passing motorist, a spark sent air-borne from an eighteen-wheeler, a heavy cumulus cloud with enough turmoil in it to cause dry lightning without creating rain, or a spark from a downed electrical line.

Every possible means of igniting a fire seemed to happen at once. Joe's ranch was burning in three places at the same time, and the ranch became a beehive of activity. Help seemed to come from everywhere—four neighboring communities' volunteer firefighters, the Texas Forest Service, ranching neighbors, friends, game wardens, local law enforcement and the U.S. Forest Service. Fire trucks, water trucks, road graders, spotter planes and C130 transport planes became commonplace for several days. At one point, Kathy was forced to seek refuge in town as the juggernaut wall of flames advanced toward her home like a tsunami being pushed on by the persistently-strong, southerly Texas wind.

She could see the advancing flames and smell the overpowering smoke. Panic set in as she quickly crammed what she could into her car's trunk, backseat and passenger seat. Joe was fighting the fire, so Kathy was terribly alone. Things she held most precious could never fit into her 2009 Mercury Grand Marquis—things like the 150-year-old hand-carved, marble-top sideboard and hutch that had been Joan's favorite piece, or the handmade grandmother chime clock that Joe's uncle build to commemorate their first anniversary. Kathy's eyes darted around the house and, like a drowning victim, she saw her life flash before her. Everything was too precious, yet she could not keep them. She must let them go, maybe forever.

Instinctively, she said a quick prayer for wisdom. Even though she was alone, she said aloud, "If God wants me to have all this stuff, it will be here when I get back." She felt an odd sense of calm as she hurriedly began grabbing whatever she could carry out to the car—clothes—Joe's favorite jeans and dress shirts and socks and underwear and cowboy boots and belts and buckles and cowboy hats. Then she turned her attention to her own closet and began snatching pants and blouses and jewelry and pajamas and underwear and shoes and more shoes and more shoes. Next she grabbed whatever medications they needed, three boxes of sterling silverware, and two of her favorite paintings done by a friend. After countless trips to the car, Kathy felt light-headed, almost giddy. The entire process took less than five minutes. "I'm either drunk or having a whale of a nightmare," she said to herself. "This just can't be real!"

Kathy took a quick inventory of the contents of the car and decided there was just enough room for her computer, so it too was stuffed into the last remaining area next to her in the front seat. "What now? I've got to get out of here." The wall of vicious flames advancing down the mesa behind her house like fire-breathing dragons terrified her. It was now merely half a mile away and gaining fast. She threw the car into reverse and started backing out of the carport.

"Damn Cat!" she shouted. "Oh, I nearly forgot the cat!" Kathy was not cussing. She was simply stating its name. Joe didn't like the cat, and he was the one that named her. "I've got to get the cat!" She grabbed a bag of cat food and threw it too into the car.

Kathy dashed back into the house to search for the cat and found her hiding, cowering, shaking like a leaf beneath the bed. The cat had been frightened by Kathy's strange behavior and had sought a safe place to hide. Complicating matters, Damn Cat was an indoor cat and had never been outdoors. She was not happy when Kathy threw her on top of the computer and quickly shut the car door.

They were finally on their way; Kathy didn't know where she was going, only that she and the cat were now refugees. Thickening smoke burned her eyes and blocked her view as she headed down the rough lane toward the highway. She was leaving her home, possibly forever, but it was all surreal. Suddenly Kathy burst into tears.

"Meeoow! Meeeooow!" It sounded more like a wounded bobcat than her cute tabby. The frightened cat quickly assessed her new territory as she searched for an exit. Like a lion in a cage, she circled the interior of the car repeatedly investigating in, around, under and over everything—crawled into the back window—didn't approve—crawled under Kathy's left arm—still no exit—crawled up onto the dash in front of Kathy—liked it. She lay down totally blocking Kathy's view.

Meanwhile, Kathy's attention had been on the flames in her rear view window. "Got to get out of here!" she said aloud and forced her attention back to now-blocked windshield. At that moment, the car hit a large rock on the side of the road and Kathy slammed on the brakes. Damn Cat slid off the windshield, still protesting very loudly, and found herself high-centered on the steering-wheel column. All four of her paws dangled helplessly. She didn't like it. For a brief moment, the startled cat stopped meowing, but quickly resumed her protestations even louder than before.

Kathy's crying instantly stopped and was replaced by hysterical laughter; she was safe and the rest just didn't matter. She still had a little way to go to reach the highway, so Damn Cat had to remain high-centered until they topped the hill and turned onto the highway.

*   *   *

Kathy and her cat spent a restless, fitful night at a friend's house in town. When Joe called about 6:00 am, she was already up waiting for his call. Her home was safe, thanks to the combined efforts of all the firefighters but especially the C130 transport pilots who bombarded the perimeter of her house with a thick, pink retardant and the road graders who cleared a two-blade-wide swath around it. She stopped by a local café to pick up breakfast burritos for all the firefighters before hurrying back to the ranch.

"Sure am glad I didn't have to wear any of this stuff," she said as she unloaded the car. "I would have looked like a clown!" The clothes in the trunk and backseat consisted of one piece of every outfit she owned. Nothing matched, but her feet would have been well-dressed. Kathy retrieved 37 pairs of shoes and put them back into her closet.

Chapter Eight
November 2014

Age and gravity had been kind to Kathy, and Joe thought she was even more attractive with her now snow-white hair. She still had a spring in her step that reminded him of the young woman deftly waiting tables in the café. Kathy not only looked good, she felt good even though she was slightly overweight. Compared to her friends, she enjoyed exceptionally good health.

Joe "wintered well" as he called it but kept his weight reasonably in-check. He still rode once or twice a week mostly because he enjoyed communing with nature. Joe always said that he felt closer to God when he was on the back of a horse.

Even the cat enjoyed good health—playful and energetic; she loved chasing insect interlopers that dared enter her territory. Damn Cat graciously allowed her humans to share her space because they fed her, but she drew the line on any other critters. She ruled her world! The cat was invincible; after all, she survived evacuation even though her tummy felt strangely tender for a few days following their road trip.

True to Kathy's promise to herself, she never looked back; she had no regrets, not even her first two marriages. Kathy reasoned that, even though they were hands-down mistakes, her marriages had led her to Joe. She was safe, secure, loved and in love. "Life just doesn't get any better than this," she told Joe one evening as they sat on the porch admiring yet another amazing Texas sunset—shockingly vivid oranges, yellows, and reds.

"Yes, it does!" Joe smiled. "You won't believe what I found out today."

Kathy nodded, encouraging Joe to keep talking. She hated it when he made her guess.

"Honey, you remember the wind turbine people that came by to talk to me about six months ago?"

She nodded again.

"Well, babe, we are getting a wind deal. It's about time this old Texas weather blew something good our way, don't you think?"

*   *   *

Short Stories

by

Gladys Dorris

Winner of "Best Overall"
Published by *Texas Federation of Women's Clubs*, Member Short
Story Contest, fall 1999

The Wet

Music drifted out from the cabin porch filling the little valley with calm. The rich vibrato of Grandpa's harmonica floated beyond the mesquite fence and did not stop until it was swallowed up by the rock-wall base of Santiago Mountain five miles away. Grandpa's nightly front-porch serenades worked magic on all within hearing. The music quieted the frogs in the water well and contented Ole Bessie in the corral. The music reached a family of javelina hogs just over the first rolling hill to the right of Grandpa Scott and ten-year-old Jeb. A ten-point mule deer raised his regal head to listen. Even the flock of wild turkeys raised their heads expectedly as Grandpa continued.

Pat, the aging cowdog, rested by the porch step. She had come to live with the Scotts shortly after Jeb was born. Half-starved for both food and affection, Pat had found both with the old man. Old man Jim Scott had christened her Cow Patty, "Pat" for short, since she was to become his right-hand helper on the old place, a small ranch close to Marathon.

Jeb chewed on a blade of grass as he sat on the porch railing, swinging his bare feet to the rhythm of Grandpa's mouth organ.

"What d'ya say, Jeb? Guess we better call it a night," Grandpa said. It was more of a statement than a question. "Mornin' comes early an' we gotta mess a' work to do tomorrow."

Jeb yawned a deep yawn and looked out over the dry, parched land. It hadn't rained for nearly four months, not since last January, and Grandpa seemed a little worried. "Reckon you're right, Grandpa. Might as well turn in."

Summer arrives early in the Southwest, especially in Texas, especially when it does not rain. Jeb had heard stories of long periods of drought from the old-timers, droughts that sometimes lasted over years, but he wasn't sure if he believed them. The drought of 1898 was said to be the worst, but that was two years before Jeb was born.

Jeb followed Grandpa into the one-room haybale house with the unusual military-sloped roof. He loved the little house. It was the only home he ever knew. His "bed" was a pallet of straw covered with cotton ticking, tucked into one corner of the room on the dirt floor. Grandpa slept on a similar pallet close to the door.

The house would have greatly benefited from a woman's attention, but Jeb did not know this. There never had been a woman in the house and he and Grandpa managed just fine. Jeb's mother died giving him life. He could barely recall his father. Jeb remembered that his father was a little awkward and sometimes fell over when he tucked Jeb in at night. Jeb wondered if his father's awkwardness had anything to do with the strange smell on his breath. It didn't matter now. Papa didn't come home one evening when Jeb was about three. Grandpa said that it had something to do with a horse and a mesquite tree. Jeb guessed that was why Papa was buried beneath the old mesquite tree out back.

Sometime during the night the rain came. The sky opened up and spilled all over Jeb's universe. Jeb figured that this was what Grandpa called a "gully washer." It rained hard and did not stop. For how long, Jeb did not know, but it seemed "nigh on forever," as Grandpa would say. Jeb lay snuggled under his cover and listened to the rain until sun-up.

After the usual breakfast—biscuits, milk-gravy, and a chicken egg—Jeb and his grandfather headed out to look for water gaps in the perimeter fence. It would take all day to do the job and Grandpa stuffed a flour sack with what he called "the necessaries"—leftover breakfast biscuits, dried beans, and Jeb's favorite, a can of peaches. Grandpa always carried his pocketknife to open the peaches. He also always carried a can of Prince Albert chewing tobacco. These too were necessaries.

Jeb's world had changed overnight. Nothing seemed to be in the same place. If it was, it looked different. More than six inches of rain had pelted the earth for more than three hours. It flowed from all the high places and filled all the lows, moving the familiar to the unfamiliar. Even Jeb's favorite "sitting" rocks had been moved by the awesome power of flood waters.

Jackrabbits and deer scampered with new vitality. Plants seemed greener and more alert; Jeb imagined that even the sotol, mesquite, catclaw and prickly pear wanted to run with the animals. Anxious for the work to be finished, Jeb wanted to walk the draw to search for arrowheads and other little boy treasures.

"Gee, ain't it great, Grandpa? Look at all the water!" Jeb imagined long hours of wading barefoot in the little lakes which were really puddles magnified by a small-boy-mind.

Pat scampered happily along behind the two humans, her dog mind distracted by every jackrabbit. Beating the air with her rapidly-wagging tail, Pat seemed to dart in every direction at once. She didn't see the snake. The rattler struck her left fore-leg and recoiled ready to strike again. Pat howled shrilly as the slumped to the ground, waiting for what she did not know. Human help arrived even before Pat's head reached the soft, moist earth.

"Grandpa! Grandpa!" Jeb cried as he cradled Pat's head in his lap. "Please help her! What can we do, Grandpa?" Tears welled up from somewhere inside and flowed uncontrollably onto the dog.

The old man looked quickly about for the snake. Even though it probably measured almost four feet long, the snake was barely visible in the shadow of a huge rock; its color almost matched the stone. The snake, too, had ventured out to experience "wet."

Making sure that the snake was a safe distance from Jeb, Jim dropped his flour sack and knelt over Pat. The dog's leg was already swelling, and her eyes seemed focused on a part of the world only she could see.

"Take it easy, girl," the old man said. "We're gonna help ya'. This here boy needs ya' around, so don't be thinkin' 'bout leaving now, y'hear?"

Grandpa fumbled in his pocket for the knife and quickly cut deep across the puncture wounds, then again, crisscrossing the first cut. Blood seemed to be everywhere, but Pat was beyond caring and feeling.

Gently the old man lifted Pat in his arms, and Jeb thought about how those same arms had lifted him up from the fresh grave beneath the mesquite. Grandpa Scott spun into action. Jeb's little legs could hardly keep up with the old man as together they ran toward the house. Grandpa laid Pat gently onto his own pallet.

"Quick Jeb, get me the lard," his voice seemed close to cracking. "It's in the cupboard by the window."

As Jeb handed his grandfather the lard, he noticed that the bleeding had almost stopped. The old man quickly scooped up a handful of lard and rubbed it directly into the open wound.

"That's all we can do fer now," he said. "Now it's wait'n see."

The next two days were the longest Jeb could ever recall. Pat clung to life, hovered somewhere just out of Jeb's reach, somewhere between life and the mesquite tree.

Jeb traded beds with the old man so he could lie next to Pat. The boy didn't have the words to express it, but somehow he hoped to transfer his own life into the dog's limp, furry body. During the third night, when the moon was high in the sky, Jeb was awakened by a strange dream. He had fallen from a horse and landed face down in cool rainwater. His face still felt wet, even though he was now fully awake.

"Grandpa! Grandpa! Wake up!" Jeb yelled with delight as he realized that his wet face had just received one of the sweetest "wets" he had ever known, a warm doggy-lick wetness that blended with his own salty tears of happiness.

Winner of "First Place"
Published by *Texas Federation of Women's Clubs*, Member Short
Story Contest, spring 2000

The Man in the Casket

A man wearing a freshly pressed pinstripe suit lay peacefully in the blue-gray economical casket. A cascade of early spring flowers seemed to flow out from all directions around the casket at the front of the First United Pentecostal Church. Friends of the deceased chatted quietly about the unusually warm weather, the fluctuating wheat prices, and the recent assassination of President John F. Kennedy. They did not speak of the deceased.

A young girl, barely sixteen years old, stood hesitantly about five feet in front of the casket. She nervously wiped her clammy palms up and down the flowing skirt of her brightly-flowered dress.

"Wear something dark, Cindy," her mother had said, and she had disobediently chosen the flowery dress. After all, she reasoned, her mother was legally blind and probably wouldn't know the difference. Flowers seemed more consistent with a celebration. And this was a long-awaited celebration for Cindy. April Fools Day seemed sardonically appropriate for the funeral of her father.

She stepped forward two short, unhurried steps, her posture exposing her uneasiness as she leaned slightly forward to look at the man's huge hands, Bernie Logan's hands finally rendered harmless. Cindy stared wide-eyed, studying the hands as one studies the formation of rattles on a freshly killed snake. Instinctively, silent tears welled up from somewhere deep inside and threatened to escape down her flushed cheeks.

"It's okay, honey. Brother Bernie's with God now as we all will be someday." The voice came from her right. Mrs. Crits, her mother's best church friend who was oblivious to Cindy's internal conflict, slipped a fleshy arm around Cindy's waist to console her grief. Cindy's breath caught in her throat as she snapped back to reality, the reality that "outsiders" saw.

"If he's with God," Cindy thought but did not say, "please don't make me go there too." She had learned early in life not to speak her thoughts.

Cindy took her seat in the front pew labeled "Family," between her middle-aged mother and her sister Shirley. The two girls were close in more ways than just age. Their friendship had endured many trials, each time emerging stronger and more unified until the girls could literally finish each other's sentences. Each knew the other's thoughts long before they were expressed.

Full-bodied notes of "Faith of Our Fathers" came from the organ behind the casket. Flowers concealed the organist making it appear that the music emanated from the corpse itself. "Faith of our fathers," Cindy repeated and wondered if he was indeed "living still" as the words of the song said. "Please, God, don't let it be so," she silently prayed.

Mr. Hillborn, Cindy's favorite high school teacher leaned over to offer his condolences. "Keep your chin up, girls," he said as the subtle, sour odor of his rain-dampened wool overcoat reached out to Cindy.

Instantly, she was back in time, transported by an ancient memory triggered by the damp wool, to a time before Cindy was aware of time. Her memory had neither origin nor ending, but rather, it had the amorphous familiarity of a repetitious nightmare.

Her knees drawn up as she cringed in the corner of her bedroom closet, she stifled her sobs with a wool coat that blocked her view of the closet door. "Stay in here," and "Stay quiet," her mother had said. "Your father will be home from work soon." Cindy could never forget the sounds of the closet—the scrape of metal on metal as the latch clicked, the silent cries that seemed to come from someone other than herself, and the muffled but loud voices from the downstairs kitchen.

"Brother Bernie passed away March 29, 1964, in a tragic automobile accident," the preacher was saying, and Cindy focused her attention on the flowers surrounding the casket. Cindy knew all the details surrounding her father's death and did not feel compelled to hear them again. Instead, she let her memories transport her to another place and time when she and her sister tried to keep warm, huddled beneath a dirty quilt in the backseat of her father's car while they waited for their parents to come out from the local bar.

"He will be sadly missed," the preacher was saying. "He leaves behind his wife, Rhonda, and his two children, Shirley and Cindy." Cindy quickly diverted her attention back to the flowers, a bouquet of white carnations crammed into a snow-white vase encompassed by a wide, white satin ribbon.

Cindy could feel the smooth, cold snow of the family driveway beneath her four-year-old body where she had slid getting out of the car. She saw her sister's arms reaching down from the icy snow bank just beyond reach of Cindy's fingertips. She could feel the weight of the rear tire as it rolled across the middle of her back. She heard her mother's screams and her sister's cries. She heard the sound of the engine as her father put the car in reverse. She felt her sister's hands inside woolen mittens as they touched her fingertips, then just woolen mittens as they slid off Shirley's hands. Too late. The car again rolled over the middle of Cindy's back.

"Just a closer walk with thee," the soloist crooned, "grant it, Jesus, this my plea" and Cindy remembered begging repeatedly for her father to stop the beating. *She was running around in circles, her left hand encased in her father's iron fist as his right arm flailed her young body with a razor strap.* She vividly recalled the need for long pants and a pillow in school to keep the hard wooden desk from stinging the welts that usually extended from her waist to her ankles.

People were moving around the church now, filing past the casket in ritualistic fashion. Most did not cast their eyes on the deceased, but chose instead to look unabashedly in the direction of their feet. Cindy sat stoically watching the line of mourners pass between her and the casket. Suddenly, she was overwhelmed with a feeling of depression, not sadness, but an overwhelming sense of having been cheated. As long as her father was alive, there was still a chance, no matter how remote, of his touching her in some way that did not produce pain.

Cindy remained seated long after all others had left the sanctuary. The moment arrived for the undertakers to roll the casket out to the awaiting hearse, and Cindy still sat as though waiting for something to occur. As the undertakers rolled the casket past her and through the side door, the wheels scraped, metal on metal against the threshold, and Cindy thought she heard the sound of the closet door opening.

Winner of "First Place"

Published by *Texas Federation of Women's Clubs*, Member Short Story Contest, spring 2002

Meme's Man

The child bolted upright in her bed as she stifled a silent, mime-like scream. Tears welled up in the corners of her dark hazel eyes. On her flushed cheeks, cold sweat glistened in the diffused glow of the streetlight outside her bedroom window. No sound emanated from her. No one noticed.

"It's okay, it'll be okay," she whispered to herself. Angela had learned to calm her own fears very early in life. She knew there were some things she could not share with her mother. One of those things was any mention of her father or his parents, Meme Jo and Abuelo Juan. The nightmare that had awakened her was of this variety.

"Mama!" she called after her voice had regained its natural velocity. "Mama!"

A small smile formed voluntarily on her eleven-year-old face as she heard the familiar slapping sound of her mother's plump bare feet on the cold linoleum of their rented home.

"What's the matter, honey?" Jessica's body appeared to fill the doorway casting a wide shadow across the small bedroom and Angela's twin bed. Her mother knew her daughter well. She sensed that something had frightened Angela awake, but did not encourage her to talk about it. "It's almost time to get up for school, Angela. You might as well get dressed and ready for breakfast. I love you."

*   *   *

"Where are my glasses? Have you seen my glasses? I can't ever find anything I need when I need it!" Jo was clearly anxious to be on her way. The red Mercury Grand Marquis was already loaded with Christmas gifts for several of her students, party snacks to share with faculty, a stack of graded essays, and a breakfast bar to eat as she drove the roughly twenty miles to town and her job. This was to be the best day of the semester. Most final exams had been graded, and she prided herself that none of her students were failing. Everything was downhill from here. The two days remaining in the semester promised to be relaxing and relatively stress-free.

"Calm down, hon." Juan handed her the glasses he found next to the bathroom sink. Jo seemed to misplace her glasses a lot lately. She misplaced her keys on a regular basis too. Once he found her keys in their bin-style deep freeze. He worried about her, but comforted himself that the Christmas break would give her some much-needed "down time."

"Thanks," she said and quickly slid past him, out the door and into her already "warmed-up" car. Juan made it a habit to start Jo's car a few minutes early every morning. It was his way of showing how deeply he loved her. He wished ranching was lucrative enough that they would not need Jo's teaching salary. Maybe West Texas agriculture would improve in the new year.

"Have a good day, hon." He threw her a kiss as she backed out of the carport and headed toward town. He watched as her taillights disappeared down the long caliche road in a cloud of drought-induced dust.

*   *   *

Jo didn't make it to school. Something happened that prevented it. Her car left the pavement, rolled over a six-foot embankment and continued rolling three more times. Mercifully, both air bags engaged, knocking Jo unconscious even before the first rollover. Not even the Jaws of Life ripping the metal door away disturbed her. She was unaware of the cacophonous police, fire and ambulance sirens.

Jo knew she had been in an accident, knew her neck was broken. Somebody said so. Jo also knew that she would not be paralyzed. Another voice, less frantic than the first, told her so. She sensed the presence of people around her as they worked feverishly to extricate her from the tangled mass of car. Jo opened her eyes briefly on the short ambulance run to town, then again on the longer doctor-ordered transfer to a bigger town. Emergency surgery was performed more than thirteen hours later, but to Jo, only three hours had elapsed.

*   *   *

Word of Jo's accident reached Angela's school via the wireless rural rumor-mill before her daddy could telephone. The school nurse drove Angela home even before the EMT workers managed to place a neck brace on her Meme.

"It's okay, it'll be okay," Angela assured her chauffeur. "Meme's going to be okay." The child's undaunted confidence almost frightened the nurse, and she was secretly relieved when they finally reached Angela's house. Her mother was waiting outside when the school car arrived.

The rest of Angela's day was spent therapeutically in her bedroom, busying herself with Barbie, Ken and her little brother's doctor bag. She never mentioned Meme's accident to her mother, and Jessica was grateful.

Although Jessica's lack of education prevented her from voicing her feelings, she viewed the accident as a nemesis. Jessica had hated her former mother-in-law for so many years, she could never remember a time when she didn't hate.

Jessica's reprieve was broken early the next morning when Angela asked to call the hospital. Reluctantly, Jessica dialed the number. The embittered daughter-in-law within her hoped the news would be bad, but the mother within wanted only news that would not upset her precious child.

"Meme? Are you okay?" The child's voice was soft and timid. Even heavily medicated, Jo could hear the love in her granddaughter's questions.

"Oh sweetie, I'll be okay. Please don't worry about me. I'm not alright yet, but I will be. I promise."

The child was full of questions, but she resisted the urge to ask them all at once. Instead, Angela settled for only one question. "Meme, I just want to know one thing. Who was the man in the car?"

"What?" She tried to recall if there had indeed been a man in the car. Nobody she could remember. "I don't know who you mean," she admitted.

"Meme, I dreamed about your accident, and there was a man in the backseat when it rolled over. Who was he?" Angela insisted.

"Well honey, I don't know," Jo said. "What did he look like? What was he wearing," thinking it was probably an EMT worker.

"Meme, he had white hair and was wearing a white suit. Was he your angel?"

Published by *Big Lake Wildcat*, weekly newspaper for Big Lake, Texas

Toppling Toilets

*H*ave you ever seen an outdoor toilet—not the modern, fiberglass, bright orange Johnny-on-the-Spot variety used on today's construction sites—but the now obsolete, wooden, two-seater model complete with a Sears catalog and a half-moon window carved in the loosely-hinged door?

Unfortunately, anyone born after 1960 probably never has seen such a noble building and almost certainly never will. Only those fortunate enough to grow up before or during the 40's and 50's can fully appreciate how much fun these unobtrusive, quaint constructions offered teenagers on Halloween night.

Luckily for me, I was one of these fortunate few although at the time my adolescent mind could not possibly fully appreciate my good fortune. Every house in my hometown, Milverton, a Canadian rural community of less than 3,000 people in southern Ontario, had an outdoor toilet so there was nothing outstanding about ours.

If at all possible, outhouses were placed close to other structures to protect the occupants from the bitterly cold winter winds common to the Great Lakes region. Ours was cleverly nestled behind the garage and in front of the chicken coop and thus it offered both protection from the cruel winds and a form of companionship. My father's Leghorn chickens never failed to greet me with scolding clucking and disapproving flapping wings when I would come flying around the corner with my flashlight in one hand and a roll of paper in the other.

One Halloween, when I was about eight years old, the outhouse took on a new meaning for me. Father was upset—literally! Some of the local teenagers had secured ropes to the back of the toilet and, while Father was busy inside, they were busy outside pulling resolutely on the ropes. His pride was the only thing damaged when he climbed out of the building which, in the moonlight, now looked to me like a huge wooden toy box with a hinged lid.

My father may have lost the battle with the toilet topplers, but the war was not yet over; he devised his own version of trench warfare. He connected a length of electrical wire to the side of the outhouse, ran it through the window at the back of the garage and secured the other end tautly to the horn of his black 1943 Ford. About four hours later, we were awakened to the loud blasting of his horn, and once the horn was quieted, we were never again bothered by the local teenagers on Halloween. After that, our toilet symbolized the forbidden fruit of my childhood.

My imagination had been ignited. The outhouse episode challenged me, and I anxiously awaited the opportunity to take part in upsetting a toilet. To me, this would be my formal rite of passage, but it was not until five years later that I got my chance.

My friends—Kathleen, Shirley and Diane—met me at the local malt shop, Mrs. A's, and we struck out on our quest for fun. Everyone halfway expected their outdoor toilet to be toppled on Halloween, and my friends and I sure did not wish to disappoint them. We were doing our predestined duty, preordained by some unwritten moral code of immaturity.

However, we had a lot to learn, and toppling toilets, like any cultural art form, was an acquired skill and required special training. Unskilled toilet topplers often found themselves in embarrassing situations, as I was soon to learn.

The weather was in our favor. It was a cloudless, moonlit night which gave us excellent visibility; no trick wires were going to interrupt our work. The temperature had hovered between 45 and 60 degrees all day and continued calm but brisk into the night. Tonight was the night, and nothing could go wrong.

Or could it? Outhouses provided me with my earliest lesson in using common sense, a lesson I will never forget.

One important aspect of this education is a thorough knowledge of the building and the surrounding terrain, knowing the enemy so to speak. Outhouses—functional but never fancy, unanchored but never unvented—were constructed of weathered, unpainted wood and required a special approach if one intended to topple them. With the exception of the seat board, which was sanded or worn smooth, they offered an excellent source of splinters. They were always situated over a roughly-dug hole about four feet deep, cleverly placed directly under the seat board for obvious reasons. This may seem unimportant but, believe me, it IS important.

Another important aspect of this education is the offensive formation of the pushers. Experienced pushers, like my three cohorts, knew that their hands must be placed on the wall of the building in order to execute the mission, as I sorrowfully learned.

We stealthily approached the building from the rear in case it was occupied, but closer investigation proved that it was empty, just waiting for us to do our duty. Shirley, Diane and Kathleen took their appointed positions against the back wall, but being an apprentice toppler and the smallest of the four girls, I decided I could best serve the team by giving backup aid. Hesitantly, I pushed as hard as I could on their backs, spreading my short arms as wide as possible to encompass all three. I was so excited by the commotion and so determined to do my very best that I completely forgot about the hole. Big mistake!

When the toilet rolled over, my friends rolled over with it; I was not so fortunate. My feet slipped in the moist earth and, before I knew it, I was face down in the hole.

Probably the most important part of these field exercises is making a speedy and undetected retreat, and this is exactly what my friends did. I found myself alone and up to my neck in education.

A slow learner, I wasn't, and after that night I joined the ranks of the experienced toilet topplers.

*G*ladys Dorris, a retired high school English, computer applications and journalism teacher, ranches with her husband in Pecos County, Texas. She was born in Canada and is a naturalized American citizen. Dorris grew up in a small, predominately German-immigrant town in Ontario, Canada. She is the 12th child in a family of 13, and has traveled throughout both Canada and the United States.

On a Wind is a fiction/romance/Christian story. While it contains a few basic correlations with her life, the story is predominately a work of fiction. Her vivid imagination, somewhat quirky sense of humor and extensive travels give her writings a unique perspective. Dorris' writings cover a wide variety of topics and genres. Her short stories and poems have won first place several times in annual State-level competitions sponsored by The Texas Federation of Women's Clubs; her work has been published in both The Texas Clubwoman and in the Big Lake Wildcat, a weekly newspaper for Big Lake, Texas.

Dorris' post-secondary education includes

- Conestoga College of Applied Arts and Technology, Stratford Campus, Ontario, Canada—business and secretarial studies
- University of Waterloo, Waterloo, Ontario, Canada—interior decorating
- Midland College, Midland, Texas, USA—Associates in general studies

- University of Texas of the Permian Basin, Odessa, Texas, USA—Bachelors Degree in literature and journalism (double major) with a minor in education
- Sul Ross State University, Alpine, Texas, USA—Masters in education
- Sul Ross State University, Alpine, Texas, USA—Reading Specialist

She graduated Magna cum Laude from Midland College, Suma cum Laude from University of Texas of the Permian Basin and Magna cum Laude from Sul Ross State University.